# BRIGID BROPHY

# THE FINISHING TOUCH

First published in 1963 by Secker and
Warburg
This edition published in 1987 by GMP
Publishers Ltd
P O Box 247, London N15 6RW, England

British Library Cataloguing in Publication
Data

Brophy, Brigid
   The finishing touch.
   I. Title
   823'.914[F]          PR6052.R583

   ISBN 0-85449-059-0

Printed by the Guernsey Press, Guernsey,
C.I.

# INTRODUCTION

I have only once put a deliberate portrait of a real person into a work of fiction, and that is not this work of fiction.

For reasons which I could trace for a psychoanalyst but which anyone else would find tedious, my temperament is anti-autobiographical. In addition, since I write both fiction and non-fiction I find it simpler to keep my fiction imagination, where you are required to invent, quite separate from my non-fiction imagination, where you are always checking dates and quotations in order to avoid accidental invention.

I do not dislike or despise autobiographical novelists: who could dislike or despise Marcel Proust? I cannot, however, be one of them, any more than I can be one of the symphonists. And to a very small extent I do despise the common academic assumption that *all* novelists are autobiographical.

What a novelist invents is seldom an entire country or an entire substitute reality, though I have made shots at doing both. Something, however, in your real reality sets your imagination going. After the fiction is written, you can, on lucky days, remember or deduce what the spark consisted of, especially if it is fixed in your mind by some external event.

In that sense I owe *The Finishing Touch* to a conjunction of chicken pox and the fact that I married an art historian.

I think that it was in 1963, when she was six, that Michael Levey's and my daughter Kate caught chicken pox. She did not feel ill for more than half a day. Michael and I escaped worry but not the tiresomeness of keeping a perfectly well child at home for what seemed weeks until she passed the infectious stage. I discovered that Michael had not had the disease during his own infancy. I counted on his good health to shield him. I had not had chicken pox, either; but I already had a rational inkling, which a doctor has since confirmed, that I possess natural immunity to it.

Kate had passed the infectious boundary and gone thankfully back to school when Michael developed chicken pox. He was beyond the advisable age and for three or four days the disease made him feel deeply ill. He simply lay in bed suffering, itching and sweating.

He recovered to the point of getting up. He could not, however, go back to his work at the National Gallery or even into the local shops because he was still a source of infection. He refused social life, even with friends who had safely had chicken pox, because most of the spots were on his face and he supposed them to make him look a good deal worse than they really did.

What did impair his looks was that he thought it wiser not to shave lest he decapitate a spot by accident and cause a pock mark. He grew a scrubby and scratchy beard, which disobligingly refused to hide the spots but circumnavigated them, leaving them sticking up like peaks; and that made him even further disinclined for company.

My immunity held through proximity to the two invalids. I felt an itch, but it was spiritual. My imagination had been seized with a novel. I yearned for time, extracted from shopping and from escorting Kate to and from school, to write it. And, since Michael was deeply bored by staying at home in the company only of a preoccupied wife, I yearned to put the finished manuscript into his hands in the hope of amusing him.

I met that private deadline by a couple of days. As a matter of fact, I that year sent a parcel containing two novels to my publisher, who decided to publish the briefer quickly, in the same year, and the longer in the next year.

As a result of Michael's assistant keepership, as it then was, at the National Gallery, I met most of the personnel of art-historical London. My part at such meetings was chiefly that of spouse/appendage, a part that leaves plenty of time for observation. What sparked my imagination to a new novel were the meetings Michael and I had with the head of an institute that taught art history. Michael occasionally lectured there and more often attended lectures by colleagues. On such occasions the head often invited us for a drink afterwards in his flat on the top floor of the remarkably elegant building that housed the institute.

Like the building, its head was remarkably elegant: in word and gesture alike. His tastes were – and that, too, was in keeping with the architecture – austere, both in relation to works of art and in food and drink. When he dined with Michael and me he became the only person I have met to refuse champagne. When we had a drink with him, which happened more often, his hospitality was multifarious but his own consumption nil.

He talked to us freely and happily about his bi-lingual (English and French) upbringing as the son of a British clergyman resident in France. There was much, it later became clear, that he did not say to us. Yet we became good, though never intimate friends with him. He belonged to an older generation than ours and generously forgave us our ignorances. He spoke in a charming upper-class drawl that was neither an affectation nor quite an Edwardian relic, and he seemed for ever on the verge of utter exhaustion. He was tall, slim and very nearly beautiful.

Whatever was concealed, there was no concealment, from us or anyone at the institute, of his homosexual affiliations. His flat on the top floor was separated from but not impregnable to the rest of the building. Whenever we went there, the evening was tattered by brief incursions of young men introduced by first name only, who might have been sailors or might have been students of Poussin and were very likely both. They would put to him practical and domestic problems ("The mustard you said would be in the cupboard on the left isn't") and he would wave a hand, dismissing not the person but the problem. Practical matters he seemed to find gross. To bend his attention on them he seemed to find impossible; the mere suggestion that he try seemed to drive him nearer than ever to the point of exhaustion.

When Michael and I came home after one of these visits we would decide in the course of discussing it that the presence of the young men in that not very self-contained flat was deliberately induced as a protective barrier, on the lines of the flitting sylphs in *The Rape of the Lock*, against more dire incursion by one of the women in the institute, who included both undergraduates and teachers, who obviously and sometimes explicitly considered him sexually desirable.

The institute, which has its handsome home in Portman Square, is the Courtauld Institute of Art. Its head was Sir Anthony (and then suddenly just Anthony again) Blunt. Everyone in the Institute had always addressed and spoken of him just as Anthony anyway.

What my imagination did, when it picked him up by the scruff of his neck, was change his sex and make him the headmistress of a finishing school for girls. Perhaps it was the hell he had imagined for himself. I notice that through all metamorphoses he retains his excellent, virtually native French and something of his adumbrated liking for sailors. He also retains his name. *The Finishing Touch* is the title supplied by my publisher, which I agree to be a better title than the one I originally wanted, namely simply *Antonia*. My publisher sent someone to search reference books for finishing schools in the south of France. Infected by the all-fiction-is-autobiographical fallacy, he was convinced I was slandering some institution where I had myself been educated and was not to be persuaded of the truth, which is that I have never set foot in a finishing school and would not know where to seek one.

Brigid Brophy
1986

# THE
# FINISHING
# TOUCH

I

Miss Braid said:

'Men are . . . coarse.'

Judging by the voice alone, you might have thought it a man who had spoken. It was a baritone, rather deeper than the average man's voice; deeper, even, than the average frog's voice.

Answering it by mistake, perhaps, the first frog of the evening called from the pool at the foot of the terraces.

'You may say it's a truism', Miss Braid went on, as though the figure sitting by the open window were incapable of supplying its own part in the conversation, 'but it's true. The note itself is . . . coarse.'

'The note.' Antonia let the words loose, as if they, too, constituted a note, in the soprano sense (middle of the register, with faintest, faintest undertones of alto). Exhausted as though she had sung a whole aria, she let her long, thin, firm, racé lips come together like the petals of

7

a flower closing for the night: a gesture of ultimate exhaustion which, at the close of this morning's reading from Racine, had provoked little Miss Outre-Mer to bury her retroussé face in her arms and convulsively write ANTONIA MOUNT four times on her mauve blotting paper.

Outside, all the frogs began to creak at once, as though at a mad dinner party every guest had simultaneously seized on his pepper mill.

'I thought for a moment you meant the note of the grenouilles.'

'I mean——' Miss Braid began in the stout voice of a sergeant-major; but Antonia held up her hand.

Miss Braid waited.

Antonia's tall, fragile figure inclined a little forward towards the open window, revealing a little of the curious story narrated in tapestry on the high back of her chair.

The evening breeze rattled across the gardens with a sound of fans, bearing the last scent of the lemon blossom. There was a pause, as for a dying man's breath. The southern night fell, like a fruit.

The frogs continued to creak in the dark.

'*Grenouille*', Antonia murmured, 'is surely the most beautiful word in any language.' She leaned back. Too exhausted to relax, she seemed to require propping in an almost military uprightness. 'Unless, perhaps, *grenadier*. Or *grenadine*. Curious that I have never liked grenadine.'

'This note which I intercepted—' Miss Braid began again; '—Antonia dear, are you sure you're not cold by that open window?'

'Well, perhaps', Antonia said. 'Perhaps'—with a gesture towards the darkness of the room—'a stole . . .'

Miss Braid rose, pulled out a drawer and began feeling inside it.

'Perhaps the peacock one', Antonia murmured, 'would look interestingly strange, almost perverse, in this crépuscule. I suppose', she added wearily, while Miss Braid spread the stole round her shoulders, 'the note is from some sailor?'

'I'm afraid so.'

'Of course, sea air', said Antonia ('*healthy climate of the Riviera*', said the Prospectus) 'is aphrodisiac.'

'Really, my dear? Do you think so?' said Miss Braid, sitting on the floor beside Antonia's feet. After a moment she leaned her head against Antonia's knee.

'I'm sure of it . . .' Antonia said, with a sigh.

They sat immobile.

'Well', said Miss Braid in her most grenouille voice, 'this won't get the chores done. The girl must be spoken to.'

9

'To which girl was the note addressed?'

'Sylvie Plash.'

'Is that the pretty one?' ('*Personal attention and care of the joint head mistresses for each girl*', said the Prospectus.)

'No, that's Eugénie.'

'So pretty', Antonia said. 'Her hair has that faint smell of fragoline. One wonders if it would taste well alla marsala. Well, my dear, you must talk to Sylvie.'

'Antonia? I was wondering if it wouldn't come better from you?'

'From me?' The voice, perfect, issued from a faint pallor in the incipient moonlight, a pallor that flinched as though from pain.

'No, no, my dear', said Miss Braid quickly. 'Of course I'll do it. It's just that I thought— coming from you—Sylvie adores you, you know.'

'O.' Antonia had cried out, wounded.

'My dear? Are you all right? What is it?'

'I can't bear '—the voice fell from agony— 'being adored by ugly girls.'

'There, there, my dear '—Miss Braid was on her knees beside the chair, half daring to rock its occupant in her arms—'you shan't be. My beautiful shan't be . . .'

'By the way', said Antonia in a wholly matter of fact voice, 'I forgot to tell you. Royalty *is* coming.'

In surprise Miss Braid let her go. 'She *is*?'

'I heard this morning.'

'When does she arrive?'

'Next Wednesday. They are so precipitate when they do make up their minds.'

'My dear, I have so much to prepare. Where do we meet her? Nice airport?'

'Worse than that', Antonia said in a dying voice. 'And when we have had so much trouble with sailors already . . . They're sending a destroyer.'

'Gosh', Miss Braid said, like a precociously voice-broken schoolboy. 'I mean'—she rose to her feet, as though for the national anthem—'it *is* rather grand.'

'The last flicker', said Antonia in a last flicker of voice, 'of gunboat diplomacy.'

'I've so much to do.' The grenouille voice was bustling already. 'I'm giving her the rose suite, the one that the Lebanese princess . . .'

'Make sure she's left none of her appurtenances behind.'

'I will *indeed*. And—Antonia? You must tell the girls. Or has it leaked out? You——'

'I shall make a small announcement tomorrow. I shall beg for their discretion.'

'I think that is very wise of you, Antonia.'

'I think—I think I should be foolish not to. In my position.'

'My dear.' The grenouille voice was moved. 'This means great things for the School.'

It would mean, Antonia thought, but without saying so, Dame Antonia Mount and Hetty Braid, M.V.O. It would obviously be that way round, even though the Prospectus affirmed the two Persons co-equal, co-eval, co-proprietors . . .

'When I think', said the moved voice, descending to bass, approaching, actually laying its arm about Antonia's stole, 'of our years together . . .'

'Sylvie Plash', said Antonia.

'O yes.' The hand dropped, the voice rose to its normal baritone. 'I suppose I'd better get it over with.'

'I suppose you had.'

'I never know what to say on these occasions.'

'Tell her men are coarse.'

'Antonia, sometimes I feel that you——'

'You're wonderful; you spare me so much', Antonia said. 'Have a drink, to nerve you before you go.'

'I never like to go to the girls' rooms smelling of drink.'

'I think you carry your scruples too far', said Antonia's faint voice in the dusk.

'Do you?'

'Too far . . . After all, their education . . . I mean, to a discreet extent . . . We are supposed to send them away *finished*. Though in some cases '—trailing; barely audible—' I prefer to think I've sent them away just *begun* . . .'

'I shall have a cup of tea afterwards', said Miss Braid. 'Can I get you a drink, dear, before I go?'

'My dear, if you would. It's a night, perhaps, for Chartreuse?'

'Yellow or green?' said Miss Braid's voice from the darkness of a cupboard. 'I can hardly see which is which.'

'Then put out both, my dear, if you would . . . I shall be drinking to your success.'

'You're so considerate of me, Antonia.'

'I am a person', said Antonia, 'who all her life long has been unable to decide whether she prefers green or yellow Chartreuse.'

Twenty-six heads bent over the School's die-stamped paper. Nineteen right hands, eight left hands (Miss Onike Rondjohns was ambidextrous) scurried along (slightly diagonal) lines. At least thirteen tongue tips protruded in concentration.

Scurrying pens on the paper made a noise like cicadas.

Outside, as the sun rose to zenith, cicadas made a noise like scurrying pens.

Looking down the table between the two rows of bent heads, Antonia reflected that this Sunday there was none of the usual search for something to write home, and noted that a girl half way down the table on the left had the prettiest pink tongue tip. The tips of the pens wrote:

'. . . de Sa Majesté la reine . . .'

'. . . Mittwoch . . .'

'. . . discreet, especially with the Press and sailors.'

Girls whose parents were divorced were issued with *two* sheets of writing paper.

As often as she dared, Regina Outre-Mer glanced to the top of the table: to the beautiful, spare features, the refined flesh, the skin which seemed always to be seen by moonlight, even when the sun was at zenith . . .

Returning to the paper, Regina's gaze fell on the words die-stamped at the left, in small discreet capitals:

CO-PROPRIETORS: MISS ANTONIA MOUNT
MISS H. BRAID

It was *almost* a signature.

Stabbed by temptation, pierced by a sudden draught of lime scent from the french windows, Regina decided to tear out the sacred three words.

14

Stealthily, muffling what her right hand was doing with her left, tenth of an inch by tenth of an inch, she ripped the words free and dropped the little oblong of paper down the front of her dress. No one had noticed. The pens all round still grated like cicadas. She wondered what explanatory postscript she could add to her letter: but it came to her that, whatever excuse she made, her family must instantly guess the truth from that tell-tale little trou, that speaking wound. 'Miss Mount?'

'My dear?'

But she called everyone my dear. Some of the girls said it was because she could not remember their names.

'Might I have another piece of paper?'

'Your parents haven't divorced, my dear?' Such a world-fatigued tenderness in the voice.

'No.' (Regina had seen somewhere an advertisement which professed to cure blushing: it could hardly be efficacious in so extreme, so fevered, a case.) 'I've spoilt my first piece.'

'My dear.' Wearily the white thin hands let one another loose from their presidential clasp on top of the mound of paper, picked a sheet, passed it to the girl on their right, who passed it on . . .

Regina received it, jealous of the hands which had contaminated it en route. How wise the

Roman rite, she thought, to practise its communions so *directly*.

They're pretty when they blush, white peonies tinged, through some error in ancestry, with crimson, Antonia thought. Yet all the same, she was weary.

She picked a piece of paper for herself, took up a pen; then paused, almost too weary to write.

This heat.

Her eyelids drooped over the paper's heading. If she became Dame, they would need a new die-stamp.

She asserted her pen.

'Hetty, dearest——'

Perhaps if they got a new die-stamp she could prevail on Hetty to appear as Miss Henrietta rather than Miss H. The girls all knew her name, in any case. Antonia herself positively requested certain girls to call her by her first name, and she was persuaded Hetty did the same. Perhaps even, in some cases, with the same girls . . .

The thought enlivened her, and the tip of her own tongue protruded a touch as she scribbled:

'I know how *fiendishly* busy you are, but *could* you come and relieve me? I think it

16

must be the sun . . . Yrs, A. P.S.', the note continued on the same line, '*could* you, when you come, count six down on the left-hand side and tell me the girl's name later?'

She folded the note, reached for an envelope from the box in front of her and then paused. Re-opening the note, she added:

'P.P.S. Also the one on the *other* side, with the retroussé nose and curls, who blushes easily.'

She put the note into its envelope and handed it to the girl sitting next to her. 'My dear, *would* you seal that for me?'

The girl's eyes sought Antonia's over the girl's tongue as it moistened the flap.

How essentially moist the girls were.

'My dear, *would* you now take it to Miss Braid?'

'Yes, Miss Mount.'

How willing, how essentially *offering* they were, how convinced that the offer of their little persons could salve . . .

'I have a slight headache', Antonia confessed when the girl was already at the door. 'You will probably find Miss Braid doing something with the *bed linen*.'

O my dear, thought Regina Outre-Mer, mentally echoing Miss Mount's own inflexion, stabbed by pity for Miss Mount's headache and her own heartache because Miss Mount was clearly sending for Miss Braid to take her place, o my dear, my dear (as if praying; as if a litany), I will never be indiscreet with the Press, or with sailors (as if promising a votive offering on condition of deliverance from storm at sea) or in any other way (forgive also those sins I have unknowingly committed or have forgotten to confess) . . . Rocking to and fro, as though tossing in storm at sea, Regina wriggled the die-stamped words in such a way as surreptitiously to caress them against the flesh of her bosom.

* * *

'The beast', said Eugénie Plash to her plain sister Sylvie as they walked beneath the limes. 'When?'

'Well, last night. At least, that's when she came to me. When she knocked, I thought it was Antonia.'

'Ah, yes', said Eugénie; 'yes, I see . . .'

Veiled, veuve-like, behind the muslin Hetty

Braid had tacked across the open window ('It's no trouble and I'm taking no risks with that headache, dearest'), Antonia looked down on her girls accomplishing that stroll before luncheon on which Hetty insisted. Hetty believed the siesta after luncheon to be an unhealthy habit for girls if not forerun by exercise before. 'It gives them an appetite.'

Yes, well I suppose it *does*, Antonia's thoughts agreed, wondering whether she would take Tio Pepe or madeira for her own apéritif.

The sun was still at zenith or even more so, if that was possible: as indeed it was: it was possible for this southern sun to clamp itself unmoving above an entire day—the long, long meridian du midi . . .

In a sense this heat was its own apéritif. Even so, Antonia poured a glass of madeira from a decanter strangely stoppered.

The Plash girls, she was pleased to notice, sensibly put up their parasols as they stepped from the shadow of the lime trees. Two pretty Plash parasols (such a well-dressed woman, their mother); beneath, one pretty Plash head, one plain . . . The girls had different fathers, of course.

The lime vista, the staggered lapse of the terracing, the pretty cupid-fountain (Hetty had insisted on a slight alteration; it had cost her some embarrassment to explain to the plumber

du midi what she wanted): Antonia's eye was
pleased. Her palate prickled likewise in a
response almost erotic to the madeira, that
liquid neither male nor female or, rather, both,
that part-deep, part-treble *glow*, that viola
among wines . . . *Fortified*, Antonia added;
one of the strongest, most vibrant, almost
bracing, of words.

A clump of girls passed, on the narrow,
gravelly path, a clump of hydrangeas. A charming sight. Which bowed?

A butterfly sought the lavender grove . . .

Antonia was not disturbed—hardly, indeed,
piqued—even by the sight of the squat young
Badessa di Poggibonsi, the only secular Abbess
(the title had been in the female line of her
family since the proto-renaissance) in all Italy
and yet all sallow bare skin (bare, that was,
but for its black hairs) and white—sailcloth,
Antonia supposed it must be; laundered to
nautical pitch, it billowed like sails over the
Abbatial podge—the Badessa picking her way
across the tiny plot where Hetty tried to grow
grass: *picking* because the Badessa was wearing,
of course, those white sandals of hers which
pained Hetty by their stiletto heels (ultimate
degeneracy into which had descended the old
high Italian custom of the stiletto) but which
offended Antonia rather by their open front
(such sallow, rounded, *wriggelly* toes had the

Badessa) and the fact that their fastening was a large white plastic daisy.

And yet, thought Antonia peaceably, it was foolish of Hetty to *try* to grow grass in a climate so plainly non-supporting of it. 'Where we live', she had already told Hetty, '*lawn* means our handkerchiefs.'

The entire view suggested to Antonia a pleasing sense of activity just sharpened by anticipation: the still, warm air hardly perceptibly quickened in expectation of the luncheon bell; bees suspended above ashy lavender flowers, the two Plash heads (with so much to discuss, of course, about the sailor and his note) buzzing together (they had settled down now, almost out of sight, behind the asparagus trenches); Hetty about to return—surely it was almost time?—from the last of her Sunday expeditions . . .

Antonia's eye discerned Fraise du Bois, the ' lady from a southern state ' (thus her guardians had described her in their letter of application) actually *in*—indeed, *flat* in—the lower asparagus trench: alas, Fraise, only nineteen and already well advanced down the slope pioneered by her cousin Blanche . . . only nineteen, twice divorced, and already registered as a narcotics addict. (The authorities were not even mean, really, in what they considered an adequate quota.) ' My dear, we must help the

21

poor thing', had been Hetty's first response when Antonia informed her that the new pupil had been accepted; later, Hetty had begun to dread the responsibility; but when the 'unfortunate child' had been in the School a fortnight Hetty confessed that she was less trouble than all the other pupils put together. 'Évidemment', Antonia had calmly replied vindicating her original decision, 'droguée as the poor creature is from dawn to dusk . . .'

Only when the bi-monthly supply was late had there once been trouble.

The Plash girls were joined by the President's daughter of what dark republic it was Antonia could never remember; but *very* dark—évidemment: the black skin, blue-damson-bloomed as night heavens, dustily moved—whispered, it seemed, visually—behind the asparagus ferns.

('I thought . . .' Sylvie Plash was explaining all over again; '. . . and then when the door opened and it was only *Braid*, I burst into tears.')

Obviously the girl took after her mother, the President. When the girl first came to the School, Madame President had unfortunately (to judge from the daughter, Antonia would have liked to see her) been too busy to escort her child; she had sent instead a withered black man, one of her Cabinet or, was it?—Antonia could not remember—one of her husbands? One, perhaps, of the girl's putative fathers? But the girl did not, certainly, resemble him.

'A natural show-case', Antonia had said when she first saw the bloomy skin, 'for jewels'. And at the School's anniversary party, the girl had appeared in emeralds (of obvious value; though rather curiously placed). Even so Antonia, though éblouie in all conscience, was not satisfied that every experiment had been made. She would have liked to try sapphires (the lucid on the dusky blue); or even, throwing away value and returning, rapturous, to nature, orchids; even, she now thought from her window, an—here; or perhaps *there*—asparagus fern. The girl even possessed, so Hetty had reported on returning from one of her tours on affairs of ménage, dusky dusting powder . . .

(But was it, Antonia prickled with the question, brown or *blue*?)

('She thought', Sylvie Plash was explaining, 'I was crying because I was sorry.')

Such a lesson, the bloomy skin, Antonia thought, for the Poggibonsian Abbess with her sallowness. But would she, in that intimate proximity behind the asparagus trench into which she was even now sinking, learn it? Would she even carry away, on her sallowness, the faintest brushing of the dusting powder? The Poggibonsian shoulders, so tightly buttoned into the white sailcloth, and buttoned, of course, down the back, disappeared; and next the white, tight Poggibonsian bottom, *also* buttoned down the back; so suggestive of the girl, Antonia thought, if *all* her clothes back-buttoned (as they well might): and also, surely?, agony to sit on buttons; or even, behind an asparagus trench, recline on buttons . . .

Horrible, square-necked white sailcloth blouse; Antonia was glad it was removed from her sight (only a white plastic daisy protruded a-botanically through the fern): a sleeveless blouse, of course: *could* Antonia ask Hetty to murmur to the squat little Abbess about possible treatments for *ses dessous de bras*? (Hetty's moment of embarrassment with the plumber *du midi* was surely sufficient years ago, sufficiently lived down . . . ?)

Miss Jones, the Monacan heiress (but not nun-like), Antonia observed, was already in her bikini again. The child was barely out of church . . .

Surely Hetty must be returning soon? It could not be that Antonia's ease of temper was going to be spoilt by—*hunger*?

Sunday morning was, for Hetty, a succession of drives, with diminishing numbers of charges. First, most sensible, most straightforward, the Catholic girls, the largest flock (quite half the pupils), with Hetty their—no, Antonia checked her fancy-rioting vision, not even the eye of

24

affection could see in Hetty a shepherdess; but their sheepdog, sturdy, reliable, brisk: the Catholic girls, in—to the town; in—to the Catholic église; out; back to the School: such a sensible, *quick* religion Antonia thought it, and Mass at such a sensible hour, too, before the sun had reached its consuming height and while a little darkening dew still lay moist on the foliage. And then, while the sun did reach its height, the Catholic girls could withdraw, already conscience-eased before the week was well begun, to write the Sunday letter home, each with a duty sensibly discharged to report, making agreeable reading for the parents. (In theory none of the Catholic girls should have been burdened with two letters home to write; in practice it was surprising how many of them were.)

Not that the Catholic devoirs had always been so straightforward for Hetty to discharge. In early days, the Catholic girls had expected to be shepherded—sheepdogged—into Nice on Saturday evenings as well, to make their confessions. The parish priest had absolutely declined Antonia's blanket assurance—even though it had been a written assurance, which surely made it official?—that none of her girls had anything to confess. Hetty had protested she could support the burden, but Antonia was determined to spare her, marbled churches

25

striking such a dangerously sudden chill on summer evenings. Besides, Antonia was not quite secure in her mind . . . Hetty was indefatigably watchful, of course, and, surely, after these years, *up* to whatever the girls might devise. And yet: no city of the seaboard could be an easy place in which to shepherd, in which to chaperone, thirteen girls in Saturday dusk. To some of the thirteen, it was true, temptation would hardly come: 'I quite understand', Antonia had said about one of these, 'if she feels impelled to implore forgiveness for her shins'. But for the others—alas if, while waiting to do so, they should *acquire* something to confess. And the Catholic religion was so peculiarly set against precautionary steps. There were, it was true, 'natural' and rhythmical methods permitted, and yet rhythm seemed not to be in the nature of girls . . . 'I fear', Antonia had sighed, uneasy in mind, 'that we shall one day find ourselves trapped between the two kinds of irregularity to which girls are prone . . .' Uneasiness was not allayed until Antonia, who permitted herself a single maxim in life ('Go higher '—pun, as it were, on her surname), consulted the Cardinal, who readily allowed that Miss Mount's girls might confess in the vacations only, when on their parents' heads be it. Hetty relieved of a chore, Antonia of an anxiety, Antonia found herself quite in charity again

with the Catholic religion (such a sensible institution, the College of Cardinals) though remaining a touch more insistent with the Catholic
girls than the others in bidding them, if they
should by chance have that capacity, satisfy
themselves with the company of their own
sex.

Even the prejudice against precautionary
measures, so potentially deleterious to the
School among the girls, militated in its favour
among the parents. It afforded Antonia a happy
sense of continuity to know that so many of her
girls, as they grew towards leaving age, had
behind them a team of little sisters growing up
to take their place, little sisters perhaps even
prettier . . . (younger children so often were
. . .). Invited to stand godmother to the newest
Cobos de Porcel girl (who made, really, one *too*
many), Antonia had even proposed a name for
the infant: Contracepción: rejected, however,
by the Cardinal baptising, Spanish Cardinals
(with the exception of Pirelli) being notoriously
narrower . . .

Even that did not put her out of charity with
the Cardinalate, whose sensibleness was all the
more to be commended when one compared it
to the Synod, the Archimandritehood, the spiritual directors of others among the girls whose
rites made of Hetty's Sunday morning, after its
straightforward start, a scramble . . . a scramble

27

to deliver the Greeks in time to hear the whole of their interminable, *unaccompanied* rite and yet to collect the Armenians before some encounter heterodox as their faith overtake them in their mosaic-floored narthex under their jewelled dome . . . and yet again Hetty must hasten to convey the single Moravian to wherever . . . Antonia had lately decided to reject, with regret (one liked the exotic), on account of the difficulty of the *day*, all Jews, Hindus and Moslems unless lapsed . . .

(She *had* accepted an Old Catholic, difficulties though it entailed. ' She does not seem to me ', Antonia had murmured, ' so very old . . .')

Surely, by now, even the last Moravian or Melchite must be being garnered in, somewhere, somewhere not far, along the Corniche . . .

In the gardens below, it seemed to Antonia, there was a restlessness. Even Fraise du Bois in her trench seemed to stir, into a kind, perhaps, of preconsciousness. The Badessa di Poggibonsi rose, still back-buttoned, from the asparagus fern and, leaving the Plash girls, began to hobble, a stiletto-heeled chèvre, up the terraces. Her breasts, Antonia thought, were vast. She could not be in milk?

Antonia must soon turn to her own Sunday duty, arrogated to herself, of searching the advice column of *Paris-Semaine* to make sure none of her girls had written. They would write, of course, anonymously: yet Antonia was confident of discerning them by their plights. Occasionally Antonia's eye would drop to the advertisements of the agences matrimoniales: '*Mr sér., sit. st., cinq., allure jeune, agr., sport. . . .*'—the answer, could it be?, for the less finished, for the less finishable girls . . . even for He—— No. Impossible thought. The School could not be run without her . . .

Only, in the gardens, little Miss Outre-Mer, whose name Antonia had lately learnt, shewed none of the restlessness of the others but sat, as she had sat all morning, disconsolate, like a poet seeking the shade, in the moist neighbourhood of the grenouillère . . . composing, perhaps, a letter to *Paris-Semaine*.

She was certainly in love. Heaven send it was not, Antonia deprecated, a sailor . . . She was such a pretty little thing . . .

The Badessa di Poggibonsi, having laboured to the top of the terraces, was photographing for the last time the chemical-coloured, faceted, pétillant Mediterranean, the mirages of water in the loops of the tarmac road (up which Hetty must soon drive), the distant glitter of the Armenian dome: for the last time because tomorrow all cameras were to be handed for safe-keeping to Miss Braid, for the duration of royalty ('the better part of discretion', Antonia had decided) ('for the duration', one said; for who could tell how long it would take to *finish* royalty?)

('I shan't hand mine in', Sylvie Plash was confiding behind the asparagus fern, the family pout which so became her sister's face disfiguring hers, ' to that old beast.')

A lizard ran over Regina Outre-Mer's wrist. Antonia, long-sighted to the point of talent, leaned forward to admire. Such a svelte, mince little wrist-bone, a rounded, perfected little knob, machine-turned, like the smallest and most accurate of gold wristlet watches.

At last the bell, thrilling through the expectant heat.

Girls rose, girls made haste, girls almost jostled . . . It was as though someone was madly throwing flowers across the gardens.

(' It's bound to be Braid at lunch ', whispered Sylvie Plash as they hurried. ' Antonia will lunch in her room, since she has a headache. I expect she'll have the melon water-ice.')

Only Regina Outre-Mer made no haste. Last, most pensive, prettiest (Antonia was becoming persuaded) . . . Antonia watched her . . . until the garden was empty.

Sighing, Antonia shook open the pages of *Paris-Semaine*, amazingly with the gesture of an old French paysan in a third-class carriage (a thing Antonia had never been in in her life). Briefly she looked through the advertisements to see if there was one about armpits which could be shewn to the Badessa. (*Paris-Semaine* in its entirety was never shewn, nor even left where the girls might come on it, but burnt, in its entirety, by Hetty.) But the advertisements were all *seins* and *poitrine*: '*C'est votre poitrine qui fascine le regard des hommes!*': the whole of this week's issue seemed given over, seemed obsessed, seemed fetichist . . .

If Hetty *brought* the melon water-ice, Antonia would accept; would, indeed, pour a little absinthe over it . . .

'*Raffermissez votre poitrine . . .*'

Really, thought Antonia, looking down, I don't think I need to. And it was true—if surprising in so lean a woman: '*une vraie poitrine de vraie femme*', as the advertisement expressed it. *And* in the right place, Antonia thought; what matter, je me demande, whether the heart is, providing . . .

II

Twenty-six girls received replies by return of post (girls who had written two letters receiving two replies).

The replies coming from such a diaspora of corners of the known world, it seemed inconceivable that *return of post* should mean in all cases the identical moment: yet by some miracles of contrivance, influence or even perhaps divine intervention (more than one prayer had ascended, more than one candle been lit, to Saint Christopher—or, with greater sophistication, to the apostle Paul himself, patron presumptive of epistles), it *did* . . . Like multivarious petals awaiting pounding into a pot pourri, the envelopes lay on the silver tray; the envelopes themselves petal-like, flimsy nautical blue, fibrous pale pink, crisp yellow, waxed white, each one stamped not merely with the normal timbres of its country of origin (though up to triple or quadruple the usual impoundage) but also stuck all over, like the vitrine of a shop

35

threatened with bankruptcy, with wild, hoping streamers—'Special Delivery', 'Express', 'Par Avion—Double'. Three or four had come in Diplomatic Bags, one or two had been delivered by hand by friends who happened to be flying . . . one had been transmitted by closed-circuit television . . . Distributed at breakfast by Miss Braid (Miss Mount took breakfast in her room), the envelopes yielded up their import at the same moment that the coffee pots liberated their morning aroma, and coffee fumes crept into the curled, the young, the faintly and in some cases quite naturally—they *were* young—scented meshes of twenty-six coiffures bent to déchiffrer the instructions from home.

'. . . tu trouveras bien sûr que la pauvre princesse, habituée à une vie formaliste et figée parmi des courtisans intéressés, aura besoin d'une vraie camarade—d'une copine même, j'ose dire—sincère, sympathique . . .'

'. . . se si può far amicizia . . . i tuoi genitori saranno contentissimi di te . . .'

'. . . d'accueillir chez nous n'importe qui des *vraies* amies de notre fille (il ne serait pas absolument interdit à ton frère de faire un mariage protestant) . . .'

'. . . might even be the means of bringing Mummy and Daddy together again . . .'

'. . . ton papa vient d'acheter une agence de presse. Il a fait tout son possible. Fais-en autant.'

⁂

'What do you think of the letter from home?' Sylvie Plash asked Eugénie.
'Antonia has asked for our *absolute discretion*. That is enough.'
'Ah, Antonia . . .', said Sylvie.

⁂

'No, my dear Hetty', Antonia murmured, giving the very faintest of shoves to her breakfast tray (Hetty's pineapple and passionfruit conserve was positively not as good this year as it had been last), 'you are *not* to wear your floral silk. One may smell but must not look like a suburban garden.' (Though for Antonia's own

37

part she preferred scents less al fresco, more d'artifice . . .)

'My darling', replied the deep factotum voice (abustle these three hours, abustle, now, in Antonia's very bedroom) 'what I shall *wear* is the least of my worries.'

'Really? It was my first consideration . . . Your poor worries', Antonia frailly added, while Hetty picked up the tray. 'You make me feel so —impuissante.'

'No, no.' Hetty set down the tray and knelt at Antonia's side. 'I didn't mean . . . My darling's not to . . .'

'Have you', Antonia exhaustedly enquired, 'had another parcel of instructions from the Palace?'

'I have, my dear. Such impossible things they seem to require. Their mind seems to run on lavatories.'

'What', asked Antonia, 'from the Keeper of the Privy this and Privy that, can one expect . . . ?'

'And I don't know *how* to fix a standard to the front of the car. And the rose suite', Hetty pursued. 'I've aired it all night, yet I swear you can still smell incense.'

'But surely only faintly', whispered Antonia, 'amidst the Egyptian tobacco and the sandal-wood . . .' (delicious).

'And the walls', Hetty said, 'are *splashed*.'

'*Splashed?*'

'Ineradicably, it seems—with some strange pale liquid.'

'No doubt she *bubbled* things through it', Antonia said.

'I should be glad if that was all. And the *bed*——'

'My dear, you make me feel a touch——'

'O, my darling mustn't . . . What a brute I am to my darling . . . My poor darling . . .'

'Hetty, I won't—I positively insist—I *won't* keep you from your work. You have so many worries . . .'

Looking in, later in the day—she had decided on her own costume, jusqu'au bout des ongles (pale pink with the faintest, she had determined, overtone of mauve)—at the rose suite, Antonia surprised Hetty scrubbing at the skirting board (such a *frou-frou* phrase, commented Antonia's thoughts), dress tucked-up in, presumably (but fortunately, as she knelt, it was not clear), her *bloomers*, hair tucked-up in a turban—which, though that is of course the last impression one wishes to give, *does*, commented Antonia withdrawing, put one in mind of a seraglio . . .

'Braid's still at it.'

'She'll be up half the night.'

'She'll be looking her worst, then, for To-morrow.'

'Ah, but Antonia won't.'

'Well of course *Antonia* won't.'

'She retired two hours ago.'

'With what book?'

'I couldn't glimpse.'

'I recognised the binding.'

'What, then?'

'*Mademoiselle de Maupin*. Again.'

'It always is', Eugénie Plash commented, affectionately, and slightly boasting of her knowledge, 'the night before an Occasion.'

III

ASTONISHING, ran Antonia's train of thought as her eye took what would be, for the time being, its last glance at the back of Hetty's neck (Hetty was just bringing the car to a halt on the quayside), that women who chose to dress like men always chose for their model the most careless, the most thorn-torn, the most ash- (or was it dandruff-?) spattered type of man . . . The drive would have been so much less fatiguing had Hetty modelled herself on some really sprucely, though not, of course, flashily, uniformed chauffeur.

Impossible, ran Hetty's train of thought as she made sure of the handbrake, climbed out and hastened to open the rear door, for an un-prejudiced observer to be sure which gave and which received honour, which came in and which was visited by state, which, in short, *was* the princess . . .

And that, of course, was just the impression, just the doubt, Antonia had dressed to provoke.

43

Leaning, as a frond might for a moment lean, on the arm extended, stepping beneath the shade of the parasol already erected and held in Hetty's other hand, she left upon the very currents of the air she displaced an impress such that air itself seemed to have sunk in obeisance about her passage and then, finding her passed, to have been set buzzing, eddying, spinning, intoxicated by the presence in it of a few volatile atoms of her unplaceable scent—which had already mis-led half a dozen lavender butterflies to follow the car, like a princesse lointaine, all the way down the Corniche into the saltier environs of the harbour, in which for them too gross atmos-phere they were doomed to die . . .

For a second Antonia paused, unable to step further——

(Was it a Tiepolo Cleopatra, come to what rendez-vous at what stately harbour, fainting away—bosom an inch exposed behind harbour-breeze-ruffled ruff—into attendant arms?)

'The drive . . . so fatiguing . . .'

'My beloved! . . . But bear up, bear up . . .'

'They might have spared us so much trouble', murmured Antonia before stepping boldly for-ward (was it now a Tiepolo greyhound straining the leash?) 'by sending her in the Diplomatic Bag. Come, to the landing-stage . . .'

'Gosh! Don't the boats look pretty? I sup-

44

pose that's what they call "dressed overall"'
(dozens of tiny coloured triangles, flapping).

'A trifle *over*dressed, admettons', said
Antonia, stepping . . .

She herself—*of course* she herself . . .

She herself (o admirable reproach to the un-
disciplined, the merely jolly fantasies of the
yacht club) did not, as a matter of fact, disdain
to borrow from masculine clothes but did so not
in Hetty's fashion—not, indeed, in any con-
temporary fashion: it was hussars (or was it
lancers?), it was a hint of mess jackets (or
*walking-out dress?*) which she conjured to mind
with the sketched allusion she made to—was it
frogging? or an epaulette here, a high collar
there? or merely a straight, a darkening line of
braid? (though not, one could feel sure, in
honour of *Miss* Braid) . . . Somehow, at least,
somehow, in giving indulgence to the dandy in
her soul (was it, then, the hint of a *stock?*) she
achieved a firm definition, a distinction, of up-
right outline. And yet, having borrowed from
the masculine (or perhaps from the travesty:
was there not, in the palimpsest of associations
she impressed on the vision, a moment's reference to Vesta Tilley?), she made it foil to the
(thus the *Paris-Semaine* advertisement) vraie
femme whose waist more than one pair of hands
had proved could be spanned by a pair of hands,
whose rib cage might have housed—might have

empalaced—the most delicate of mechanical singing birds, whose *vraie poitrine* was calibrated with the architectural perfection, the touch of the glacial and yet the tender suspicion of the meltingness and (last, most poignant suggestion of all) the very ephemerality of twin domes of water-ice . . .

All this, the hint of uniform, the material shiny and *ribbed*, its colour—what colour? dark . . . a changing colour, colour of a moody sea, the wine-moody sea—all this not merely offset; it actually, it openly, it all but blatantly revealed. For somehow, somewhere, the top was actually (the principle of all works of art:- excise) *cut away* (mess jackets, cut-aways . . . ) And yet it *was* only *all but* blatantly, for what was revealed was by the same art withdrawn: bosom, throat, hair ('I, at least, shall not flap in the breeze'), the lovely face itself . . . all lurked behind—not *a* veil but veiling, veiling without end and without beginning, mystic symbol of eternity . . .

How, then, to tell, as she stepped, head and shoulders swathed in her veiling and her scent, *which* was royal? (Antonia affected even the royal dislike of carrying money and doing one's own paying: her handbag followed after in Hetty's hands—*handbag*, one said; it was the merest little gold sack of netting, just deep enough to encompass the small lavender-suede portefeuille; delicate—in the square, slightly embarrassed hands—almost to the point of évanouissement.) Antonia did not fall short even in entourage. The car which had followed (Hetty glanced back, through the nimbus of Antonia's scent, to make sure it was keeping to its schedule) bore three, as it were, maids of honour. 'They shall be my nosegay', Antonia had said, 'my sweet-smelling orange stuck with cloves'—and, to make her promise good, had, before leaving the School, touched each girl behind the ears with a benison of—whatever it was; each girl had guessed at the scent; each guess had been wrong.

Hetty had assumed the three girls would be selected according to precedence, after consulting the Almanach de Gotha; but Antonia had employed some other principle; the three were Eugénie Plash, Regina Outre-Mer and the President's daughter of the black (the damson-blue) republic.

('My dear, are you sure?' Hetty had murmured about the last choice.

'My dear, surely she's used to it—from the *Commonwealth*?')

Hetty glanced back again, to make sure the girls were following. Antonia had no need. She recognised her scent.

She stepped . . .

She stepped *up* . . . Up, on to the floating

landing-stage, which was got-up (dressed overall, no doubt) for the occasion : more triangles flapping, some effort towards cushioning the slatted benches and, at the other—the *waterside*—entrance, where SHE would presently appear, two pots of hydrangeas, which lurched with the landing-stage. 'One can't help feeling *safe*', Hetty cheerfully said, 'with the Navy'.

The Navy—a sous-officier, in tropical kit—saluted.

'Commander Curl presents his compliments.'

At least, Antonia reflected, if I get my damehood, it will be without strings.

(Apparently the sous-officier had meant Commander Curl was coming. Qu'il vienne, then.)

They cannot expect me to attend a Garden-Party. No party could—surely?—be the *better* for being held in a garden? But of course it was not meant to be. The institution was merely a British perversity (almost a sexual perversity), a flirting with the climate they did not possess, just as certain women who did not possess the figure for trousers felt compelled . . .

Commander Curl.

O dreadful, dreadful tropical kit, the white socks long and the white trousers short (men as well as women might not possess . . . and for them, no choice), uniform one would expect to see directing the traffic from a white tub in Morocco . . .

Two fingers, two fingers only, to him . . .

' You had a pleasant voyage, I hope? '

' O—great fun.'

' Fun? '

' Lots of jolly deck games.'

' How fatiguing. Do sit down.'

How curious of him to appear disconcerted, to merely mumble there was hardly time, the royal launch . . .

And yet in a way, when he blushed (reminding one of little Miss Outre-Mer), there was a charm . . . A charm, even, in the absurd uniform, in revealing the knees (could they be made to blush?) Pleasure could be derived from these northern complexions (so easily blushing for one thing) which took so ruddily to southern sun . . . Had one been unfair? too long expatriate? would one, in effect, rather welcome the complexion, the dewiness, of an English rose . . .?

The royal launch: in sight: hove to: tying up . . .

Now heaven send the Commander was delivering up his cargo as he had received her (*did* one feel safe with the Navy?) . . .

She.

(Of course he was. That was perfectly obvious.)

She was not an English rose.

But she—her—not dress: covering—*rioted* with them.

A long, long tremor, a shuddering, a rigor passed through Antonia into Hetty's arm. 'My beloved . . . my beautiful . . . you've borne up so bravely . . . don't fail now . . .'

(Remember to bid Hetty, when occupied with affairs of ménage, to look for the label: C & . . .)

'Smashing trip! Smashing to see you! Smashing . . .'

But it was one of the hydrangea pots . . . smashed indeed . . . its fragments irrecoverable as the treasure ships of Phoenicians and Greeks beneath the wine-moody surface of the Mediterranean Sea . . .

'Smashing place you've got here. Smashing grounds. Smashing *view*.'

'A touch, I fear', Antonia murmured, 'banal.'

'Do you think so?'

'Colour photography has spoilt so many pleasures. Sometimes I wish for days together they would invent spectacles that corrected the vision to black and white.'

For royalty Antonia herself must conduct the tour of the gardens. How long since she had actually set foot in them? But then what need, when she had her talent of long sight?

But now—for royalty—What a clamber it was to the top of the terracing: and to be rewarded by the merely banal view. And from royalty, she supposed, one could not even expect an arm.

Girls, it seemed to Antonia, were with them, though not accompanying them; all round them, though not visible to them: girls scuttling like lizards (and as prettily) across the path one was about to take, girls hovering like humming birds in the grove one had just left: girls naturally eager, no doubt, to catch their first glimpse of their new, their royal, companion . . .

Or was it to see Miss Mount that they lurked?, Miss Mount so unaccustomedly, so actually *in* the gardens? Well no doubt that, too, and equally naturally, had created its furore: Miss Mount displaying the grenouillère (royal joke about frogs), Miss Mount disclosing the nectarine wall (royal knowledgeableness about pruning), Miss Mount holding erect her own parasol (for Hetty, of course, was unpacking the thirty-one pieces of royal baggage, each one yielding up, no doubt—Antonia suffered a moment's return of her quayside rigor—its own Horror of Glamis) and remembering from time to time to correct its angle so that a little of the shade from its fringes dripped over royalty's head . . .

But though one might not expect an arm *from* royalty one might tactfully touch one's own hand to royalty's elbow and divert the gaze which had been on the point of penetrating the hibiscus and lighting on the statue of Pan. (*That* Hetty had not been able—or had not dared —to have corrected.)

(But was it not down that very avenue—and not inappropriately—that Antonia glimpsed a flicker of orange and bacchic purple, strong tropical contrast that could only denote the sundress of the President's daughter? . . .)

'But I say——'

(There: that jewelled flicker in the ilex leaves: was that not Regina Outre-Mer?)

'——where are the playing fields?'

'The playing fields?'

'For games, you know.'

'O, as for games, the gardens are admirably adapted to them. So many secluded corners, sunken spots, grottoes one would never guess were there . . .' Antonia replied, wondering, rather, that the royal child could not see as much for herself.

'Yes, but I mean to say. For rounders, you know, you need a flat bit.'

'A flat bit', Antonia echoed. 'There is—' she sighed, beginning to lead royalty there, '—a small plot which my colleague has attempted to engazonner.'

Wearying, Antonia thought (having again the sense of girls scuttling from sight before the royal advance), this impression it makes on me of being cut off, as though the shadow of this parasol (remember to lend a little of it to royalty) were an impalpable cage, keeping me from my girls . . .

'There', Antonia said. 'Miss Braid's pelouse.'

A flat bit, her thoughts echoed again. It seemed to express.

'O, I say.' Royalty giggled. 'Sorry—but it is a bit of a pocket handkerchief, isn't it?'

'But one's pocket handkerchief', Antonia said, fatigued, '*is* lawn.'

I am tired, Antonia thought; I am repeating my jokes; tired . . .

With a premonition of headache she decided to accord royalty no more shade but to keep it all for her own incipiently pained head . . .

'My beloved must be so tired.'

'It is always tiring when one fails to discern a single charm.'

'I must admit she isn't in the least——' Rarely, rarely did Hetty fail to complete a sentence: so sturdy, so reliable she was. If Hetty becomes depressed, thought Antonia, I shall simply give up; the School must close . . .

'—pretty', completed Hetty. The School might continue . . .

'Her face is a touch—no, it is quite distinctly', Antonia pronounced, almost with vigour, '—oxyrhinque. Indeed, she all too indomitably does', Antonia added, *keep her pecker up.*'

And after dinner (even the melon water-ice was failing now):

'My poor tired beloved must go straight to——'

'I have my Report to write first.' (They expected one a day. But this task could fairly soon, Antonia thought, be passed to Hetty.)

'H.R.H.'s French', Antonia wrote, 'is fluent, wide in point of vocabulary and of a perfection in point of accent: H.R.H.'s mind seems, however, innocent of French Literature.'

'Well, what can you expect?' commented Hetty, handed the Report for sealing.

54

'What indeed? One can only faire son possible.'

'Rest now, my beloved; try to rest.'

'Tomorrow I shall start a special Literature group. A small group, I think . . . informal. We shall meet in my study. The President's daughter, I think, Eugénie Plash and, perhaps, Regina Outre-Mer.'

'And H.R.H.'

'And H.R.H.—I was forgetting', sighed Antonia. 'How readily does one retire—from the *stress*—into one's fantasies.'

'My darling shall do no more work tonight', whispered Hetty. 'Can I help my darling undr——'

'No, dear. You must get the Report in the Bag. I won't detain you.'

'Then . . .'

'Then . . .'

Strange how, even when one was left alone, the usual pleased embarras of choice in solitude had yielded place to a desert of discontent. Parched though one was, none of the springs . . . The Grand Marnier bottle merely grossly bulbous, worthy of cooking only, the very Bénédictine suggesting none but the schoolgirl interpretation of its ciphered D.O.M., even the green and the yellow Chartreuse bottles, so resemblant yet so disparate, sister-bottles, alcoholic Plash girls, failing to tempt . . . Was

one, then, old? or ill?—or death-wishing?
Strange this, in the ultimate reaches of fatigue,
masochistic longing for oblivion, this wish to be
hit, to be coshed, to be slugged, actually, over
the back of the head . . . Had one indeed been
too long expatriate? Could it be that today had
stirred home thoughts, that one was wishing for
one's native . . . ? Self-astounded, all but
ashamed, Antonia poured (and added no water)
a cut-glass tumblerful of Scotch . . .

IV

By some oversight, although there were five persons (Antonia, her nosegay, H.R.H.), there were only four copies of the text.

(Antonia had decided to read with them some poems of Renée Vivien.)

Who, then, should share Antonia's copy?

*Not* H.R.H., whom Antonia had already placed in an arm chair which was in fact deeply comfortable and would therefore pass for the place of honour, but whose arms, rendering the occupant all but besieged, made unthinkable any encroachment of sharing . . . It was placed, this chair, at the furthest remove from Antonia's own; even so, Antonia expected to undergo some suffering by virtue of her long sight . . .

*Not*, Antonia decided, Eugénie Plash . . . Ever since Antonia's notice had been drawn to Sylvie Plash, she could not prevent herself from remarking that there was between the two faces an extreme familial resemblance. Indeed, it would be hard to point any more than subjec-

59

tively perceived distinction: no doubt if one took a measuring rod to the two there would turn out to be virtually nothing in it . . .

It lay, therefore, between the President's daughter and Regina Outre-Mer.

Ever since Regina's own demonstration had been reinforced by Commander Curl's, Antonia had borne in the front of her mind the prettiness of blushes and the pleasures of provoking them. If the President's damson daughter *had* a defect —and she must be allowed one; she was only human (surely?)—it was that she *could* not— well, one could not, naturally, *expect* her to . . .

It was, therefore, to Regina Outre-Mer that Antonia frailly signalled a small patting gesture of the air beside her; Regina who sank (how prettily) on to the rose-pink, rose-soft carpet at Antonia's pointed feet; Regina whose bent head indicated she was blushing already (but she must look up if she was to see the text; meanwhile, how appealing the chrysanthemum top presented to Antonia's view).

Royalty, of course, did not mind: did not notice. The President's daughter noticed but seemed not to care. (I think, Antonia remarked to herself and felt sad at the thought, she was never really interested in the first place; perhaps —ah, a second's faintness at the heart—these girls from torrid countries are, ultimately, cold . . .) From Eugénie Plash's pout Antonia turned away. It put her in mind of Sylvie.

Regina Outre-Mer's arm lay alongside, lay almost touching, Antonia's. Regina's little wrist knob turned, wriggled, darting as a lizard, scintillating as a jewelled watch, this way and that, in embarrassment? in pleasure?, distracting Antonia's eye from Renée Vivien . . . O, most poignant of little poignets . . . Yet one could not very well, beneath the staring face of royalty (deep-puzzled by Renée Vivien), lean forward to kiss it . . .

V

H ETTY'S MIND became a teeming womb of royal hazards.

Every day, every hour it seemed to Antonia (already wearied by the high summer heat), Hetty's imagination gave phantom-birth to another catastrophe. Not alone the real dangers of press photographers (Hetty had had to throw stones at one before he would climb down from the garden wall; flapping her arms had made no effect) and sailors (both the native ones with their absurd red pom-poms on their hats and the British with their absurd naked knees twinkling —because *peeling*—like pink pom-poms)— though in fact Antonia judged royalty unsusceptible to the advances of sailors—or anyone else; the most far-conjured eventualities rose to frighten Hetty in the night and, in the morning, pale over Antonia's breakfast tray (so offputting —even if the pineapple and passionfruit conserve *had* been of her best), she would offer:

Suppose royalty should fall into the sea?

65

Suppose royalty should contract la grippe?

Suppose the cuisine should not agree with . . .

If royalty *gets* la grippe, thought Antonia—a far worse hazard was that Hetty should lose hers.

Why should Hetty now flinch from her share of the responsibility (if Hetty fails, I shall simply lay down my burden) when Antonia had borne hers? Hetty had no need to flinch: she was so perfectly competent. (Surely Hetty *was* so perfectly competent? One had not been entrusting one's affairs these years to one who was *not*? . . .)

Suppose royalty were to fling herself from the window of the rose suite?

'But why *should* she, my dear? She is surely not in love. And I know of no other pretext.'

'No, no, you're quite right, my darling's quite right. I'm just being a silly. I'm a little moithered these days. Perhaps it's the Mistral coming on.'

'Every emotion on this coastline', Antonia sighed, 'is attributed to the Mistral's coming, being overdue or having just gone. One would take it for a function of feminine physiology.'

Hetty permitted herself to look wounded.

'There', said Antonia delicately, 'there. Have a drink.'

'No, no, my dear' (but kindness in Antonia's tone was stronger stimulant) 'I need my wits about me.'

Of Antonia's world-tired smile Hetty would never be certain of the import. But she chose to read it kindly.

And yet:

'And yet', said Hetty, pausing on her way from the room (I hope, Antonia thought, she *has* her wits about balancing the tray), 'supposing she fell by accident?'

'My dear, the *Lebanese* princess managed perfectly well about staying inside.'

As a matter of fact, the Lebanese princess had tossed several exotic objects from her window (and one or two erotic) but never, so far as Antonia knew, herself (who had been both).

'What do you think of her?'

'I think she's the loveliest thing I've ever seen', said Regina Outre-Mer.

'*Do* you?' said all the girls, deep-surprised.

'Whom', Regina asked, suddenly égarée, 'are we discussing?'

'Royalty.'

'O. O, I thought you meant——'

'We haven't all your obsession', said Eugénie Plash.

But her nastiness of tone went unnoticed by Regina, who simply replied, wonderingly:

'Haven't we? How strange people are.'

Suppose a lizard bit royalty?

'*Can* they?' Antonia replied, with scepticism enough to convince Hetty they could not.

But a mosquito could: a hundred mosquitoes could: worst of all, the local wasp, the dreaded guêpe du midi, whose venom, if not extracted from the bloodstream within twenty minutes . . .

'My dear, I'm less afraid', Antonia faintly said, 'of what she may suffer than of what she may inflict.'

'Come', said the baritone roundly, 'she's not exactly a breaker of hearts.'

'Not of hearts', said the soprano, tremolo (the tremolo alone tinged with alto) . . . 'Did you lock up the Dresden?'

'My dearest, yes, but——'

'And not' (diminuendo) 'in the glass-fronted cabinet? . . .'

'No, my dear, but I think you exaggerate the——'

'Exaggerate!'—frail cry, like the splintering

of frailest porcelain. 'But you *saw* that hydrangea pot!'

'My loveliest, she really and truly has smashed nothing since.'

All very well for Hetty, who (*was* she losing a little in reliability?) retained at least her sturdiness, but when one was oneself of a Dresden fragility . . .

(Remember to push one's chair, at the study group, to a yet further extreme from the royal chair. What matter if one's faint voice failed to carry to royal ears? They could hardly take in less than they did . . .)

To remove one's chair yet further from royalty meant to withdraw yet deeper into a recess (taking, of course, Regina Outre-Mer in one's train).

Here sunlight (filtered, of course, in the first place, through venetian blinds) had scarcely the strength—or the heart?—to reach. Here one was—here two were—swathed in a veiling pénombre. Regina, if she was to *see* the text laid on the soft lap, must——

'Lean closer, dear child', Antonia murmured; 'do not feel shy . . .'

And Antonia, if she was to *see* the pretty blushes her murmur provoked, must, in her turn . . .

The text, as a matter of fact, was no longer the same. Royalty making so little of Renée Vivien, Antonia had substituted something simpler (*Albertine Disparue*, as a matter of fact) . . . As it turned curiously out, there were only four copies of this, too . . .

('Poverty', Eugénie Plash unpleasantly commented afterwards, 'seems to have overtaken Antonia's library'—unpleasantness again lost on Regina Outre-Mer, who, kissing her own little wrist which, for one moment of page-turning, had actually rested on Antonia's lap and smelt now of Antonia's scent, clasped to herself the mental exclamation Holy Poverty!)

Almost invisible to her pupils, almost inaudible to the further flung of them, Antonia yet presided . . . by the distinction of the frail silhouette, by the sighing of her frail dress, by the frail authority with which she turned the pages (when Antonia turns, we all . . . as though, vulgar thought!, we were all in a vast feather bed . . .) She looked, presidingly : from the indifferent face of Madame President's daughter (Antonia was sure, now, such girls were cold) to the baffled face of royalty, staring straight ahead as though air rather than the text could help her understanding, to the cross face of Eugénie Plash—— Look away quickly (heaven grant I am not to suffer a headache today), look back to the text, look down at . . . and thus, naturally, to let one's gaze slide off the text, slide off one's lap (pleasing though that was to look at), to alight . . .

From where Antonia sat, Regina's lovely shoulders, throat, collar bone extended themselves beneath Antonia's vision like a model of physical geography . . . ah, deux collines . . . There was a place, whiter than the rest because only just, with the coming of extreme summer, had Regina taken to the extreme of the sundress, a place just rising, yet firm, and yet again tender . . . a place to which Antonia's vision, sliding from the text, was naturally directed, to which Antonia's lips, if Antonia herself were to slide forward—she had only to lean a little forward, a little down . . .

The President's daughter obediently if indifferently following her text; Eugénie Plash so disgruntled as to be doubled over hers: only royalty staring straight in front of her, uncomprehending. But could one rely on her uncomprehension—of everything?

Antonia had only to bend a touch forward.

(Invisible as I must almost be . . .)

If only royalty would——

'I think we should keep *closely* to our texts . . .'

Girls bent closer to their books, even Regina (I did not mean *you*, my dear), chrysanthemum head obscuring the spot . . . no, it appeared again, tempted again . . .

Only royalty made no closer application, stared still ahead. She had perhaps, remote as one had put her, not heard. But would she *see*? seeing, comprehend? Could one *rely* . . . ?

Ah, one could not, one could not . . .

ah, ache . . .

Naturally, when the Palace telephoned in the middle of the night, Hetty was assured of disaster.

'My dearest—ah, what a shame to wake my love—but my dearest, my loveliest, they want *you*.'

Fortunate that Antonia's nightcap had not this time been the oblivion-creating, the slugging Scotch.

'What is it?'

'My dear, I don't know, but I feel sure—o, be brave, my love—that it's *serious*. Perhaps they want to withdraw her. Perhaps they've *heard* something . . .'

'What', Antonia asked, graven pale on the lilac pillow, 'could they have heard?'

'O, my dear . . .' Hetty stared down at the perfect face. It sometimes seemed to her that her memories of the past did not coincide with Antonia's, even though it was a common past. 'My love, whatever happens, I will never desert——'

'Switch it through here', Antonia frailly interrupted. (Telephone calls in hours of darkness went to Hetty's room.)

'Yes, my love. Let me just prop my love's pillows up before I go . . .'

Antonia reached, sleep-handed, for the receiver.

'Allô, allô?'

(They are presumably knowledgeable enough not to confound me with a woman who would drop her h's?)

'Hullo? Miss Mount? Office of the Keeper of the Privy——' (whatever it was: he mumbled the word: it could not have been *privy*, bis?) 'here'. (Jolly male voice; grating, in these small silent hours, as a football-match-rattle in the ears.) 'I say, I hope I'm not ringing too late? Thought I'd better wait till SHE was asleep.'

'SHE', echoed Antonia. (But *I*?)

'H.R.H., you know. Just wanted to check up, you know—how you're rubbing along?'

'We're rubbing along', Antonia breathed (lasse, lasse . . .) 'very well.'

'Top hole. No worries then? First chop.' (But I lack the stamina for this so *fade* slang in the small hours.) 'Just wanted to make sure you were finding——'

'I find her', Antonia feebly loosed the words, 'smashing.'

'She *is* a jolly girl, isn't she? And quite unspoilt.'

'I fear only for what she may spoil.'

'I beg your pardon?'

'The line . . . seems almost failing.'

'I'll speak up a bit, then.' (But *can* you speak louder—and still be human?) 'Just wanted to—— O, by the way. Your first Report's arrived. Jolly good. Thought I'd just let you know it'll be passed on tomorrow. I mean: it'll go higher, don't you know?'

'My very own motto', murmured Antonia, en raccrochant.

'My love?'

(Had you been lurking, then, not daring to open the door?)

'My love, my poor love, I hardly dare ask . . .'

'Calm yourself, Hetty, je t'implore—it was,

74

by the way, nothing—and, if you would, lay
my pillows flat again . . .'

'If you ask me, she's simply dim.' But the
President's daughter, as President's daughter of
a Republic, was perhaps ex officio prejudiced
against royal persons.

'Makes nonsense of Antonia's imploring our
discretion', said Eugénie Plash. 'She simply
wouldn't get it—if we *did* tell her about
Antonia.'

'Tell her *what* about Antonia?' enquired
Regina Outre-Mer.

'. . . *what* about Antonia?' mimicked
Eugénie.

'You don't mean Antonia—*drinks*?'

Let them giggle. Regina loved.

VI

THE ROYAL ARMS: embossed (making, one had to admit, quite a prettily heraldic effect against the silver breakfast tray).

*Office of the Keeper*, etc., etc.: stamped.

But, beneath that, sad degeneracy of a merely schoolboy (polite name for illiterate) scrawl with a ball point:

> ' Just to let you know the reaction—They are jolly pleased with Report—Glad to know you find H.R.H. innocent and are not letting her read French books.'

One is, thought Antonia, smoothing the frilled sleeve of her breakfast négligé (pale: it was not the hour for strong colour), misunderstood.

VII

‘I HATE to worry my beloved when she has cares enough already——’

‘You have not imagined another royal catastrophe?’

‘No, my beloved—though it did cross my mind, now she has induced some of the younger girls to play rounders——’

‘So energetic, the blood royal . . . And your poor pelouse.’

‘For the School, I don't mind—— But if a stray ball *should* smash——’

‘The boot, my dear Hetty, is surely on the other foot. Let her not, at all costs, drive the car.’

‘No, *indeed*. It wouldn't be safe——’

‘Indeed, without the car we should be *lost* . . .’

‘—when the roads are so full of sailors . . .’

—‘Practising, no doubt, l'auto-stop. Yet I am more worried lest she *couldn't* stop. But what . . . ?’

83

'It's Sylvie Plash, my love.'

'La grippe?'

'The sulks.'

'I feel no sympathy.'

How indeed could one feel sympathy, when Sylvie, by the existence of her face, had spoilt for Antonia her sister's?

'She's retired to her room.'

'Then one need not see her.'

'You couldn't possibly speak? She hates *me*. But a word from you——'

'Eugénie might be asked to reason with her sister . . .'

'Excellent idea. My beloved is so practical. My beloved could not bear, herself, to ask Eugénie . . . ?'

*Could* one? A little private interview with the face that had once held charm? No; horrible superimposition of that other, that so resembling, face . . .

Seeing the shiver which ran through Antonia's arm, Hetty reached her hand out to calm it. 'I'm brutal even to have suggested it. Of course my darling shan't.' The tremulous arm accepted the touch; shuddered into stillness.

Hetty's competence did, one admitted, have a certain power to calm. It always had had.

'We have our memories', said the beautiful, the Dian-pale face.

So she *did* remember.

84

Hetty's touch firmed.

'But I mustn't detain you, my dear', said Antonia, sighing with self-abnegation.

<hr>

'She's *so* dim', pronounced Eugénie Plash, 'she wouldn't get it even if we told her about *Antonia and Braid.*'

<hr>

'One is', Antonia repeated, this time aloud (she had just shewn Hetty the letter with the embossed Arms), 'misunderstood.'

'Ah, my dearest', Hetty responded, voice more than usually profondo, face more than usually tombstone oblong, in compassion. 'Sometimes, my loveliest, I fear . . .'

'What, Hetty, now . . . ?'

'That that is your doom, my love—to be misunderstood.'

'How many premonitions you have these

days . . . Well', said Antonia, resignant, brave, 'if it is one's doom . . .'

'What nonsense I'm talking.' Hetty obliged her voice back into its normal, its jovial baritone. 'Silly Hetty, frightening her love.'

'And yet', Antonia bravely pursued, 'one must, in effect, face some small ironies.'

'My love?'

'The child—the royal child, I mean—could not well have learnt less about French Literature if it *had* been my intention to keep if from her.'

'O my dear—and you have laboured so nobly. My dear, I do occasionally wonder—it *has* just crossed my mind—— My love, do you not perhaps think that for a beginner, for such an absolutely unsophisticated intellect, *Albertine Disparue* is just a little hard?'

'Hard . . . ?' (Surely the hardness was to imagine a state of mind where it could be hard?)

'Just a little complex? A little subtle?'

'And yet', Antonia mused, 'it seemed to me, on re-reading it, almost too grossly blatant . . .'

'It is so difficult for my love to come down from her heights.'

'Am I then to be forced', asked Antonia, all but failing, 'to use a bludgeon?'

'O my angel, not *forced!*' (pierced, the deep voice . . .)

86

'Forced', Antonia affirmed, all but à bout de (*her*) forces.

'O my angel!'

'If I must', Antonia breathed, 'I must. Be so good, Hetty, as——'

'My angel?'

'—to put out four copies—'

'Four copies, my angel?'

'—of' (let not the ultimate shudder overwhelm, quite, the words) '*Claudine à l'École.*'

And yet, before the sun had climbed, quite, to its ultimate, torridest zenith (exaggerating by contrast the cool pénombre in the depth of Antonia's study) Antonia was reconciled to *Claudine* . . . It had made Regina Outre-Mer laugh.

And yet again, deep in the chill of the never quite completely obscure Mediterranean night,

' Is my beloved still sitting up? '

' I cannot sleep ', Antonia simply said.

For there had been—although the chrysan-themum-petal hair had shaken under the impetus of an only half-suffocatable giggle, and although that tender, white, kiss-tempting, kiss-inviting spot above the bosom had quivered, like a delicate yet fleshy leaf ridding itself of a last raindrop—there had been, there had *still* been, no opportunity . . . For royalty, as uncomprehending of the comic as of everything else, had again sat, graven, staring straight ahead . . .

' My beloved is brooding—are you not?—on her special Literature class? Tell Hetty.'

' It fatigues, it troubles, I confess . . .'

' *There*. Hetty *knew*, Hetty knew. Ah my love, what you sacrifice for royalty.'

(What indeed.)

' If only *they*—at the Palace, I mean—realised . . .'

(If only they did.)

'—it would be far, far more than *Dame*.'

(So Hetty *had* divined what would ensue? At least, Antonia's thoughts appended, I think my *Dame* will become me. It goes quite—trochee, dactyl—hexametrically with *Antonia*. As for the pantomimic associations of the word, few so well equipped as I to live them down—or, rather, put them clean out of court, stifled before born . . . Whereas, if they were to give one to *Hetty* . . .)

'My love *shall not* be troubled. She shan't indeed. Now climb into bed, and let Hetty tuck——'

'No.'

'Antonia.'

What could one, utterly at the end of one's strength, reply?

'*My* Antonia . . .' (but tentatively, testing out the proprietorship, as though fearful for it . . .)

'Forgive me, my dear. I am the prey of a certain—nervosité.'

'Perhaps it's the——' Hetty stopped, remembering what Antonia had said the last time she mentioned the Mistral. 'Be brave, my darling. It will pass.'

'Tout passe . . .' (The *sadness* in the voice!)

'My darling! Perhaps—a little nightcap?'

'Even that, somehow, tonight . . .'

'I could warm you a little milk.'

'No, no.'

'I hate to leave you like this——'

(Yet you must: one's nervosité can really endure no more.)

'I am so worried——'

'Let me not keep you up, too, Hetty. It will,

as you say, pass. A merely momentary, a really negligible, a really too petite crise. I am better to suffer it alone.'

'But how can I bear——'

'My dear, I am only' (ah, devouring tiger at the heart) 'a little under the—' (no; even in torment let one not be betrayed into that vulgar, that characteristically meteorological English expression) '—à l'ombre, mettons.'

'Ah, but of *what*?' cried Hetty. 'If only my beloved would tell me *precisely*.'

'—des jeunes filles en fleur, je suppose', completed Antonia, but only as the door was closing . . . closing . . .

Closed. At last closed.

Now prowl, tiger. Now lash, gnash . . .

. . . but soundlessly. Not a moan, not a pacing, not a laceration come to the ears of the rose suite.

Unrelenting desire . . .

You are caged, tiger, au delà des grilles (desire unassuageable), prospective damehood the gaoler; as good as locked-in to your pretty, flowery, quilted boudoir (o quilted irony) . . .

Howl

. . . but silently.

And yet: and yet who am I, Antonia Mount, virtually Dame Antonia Mount, to submit to a key which has not factually turned?

Look, I can open my door (relent, tiger; you

shall be assuaged). Look, I can open it as softly as dew visiting flowers, as softly as my lips will . . .

At least, thought Antonia, paused but a pace from Regina Outre-Mer's threshold, if I am making (inelegant phrase!) a fool of myself, I am doing it in the most becoming conceivable nightdress. If royalty should choose at this moment to open her rose door and look out——

But no door opened.

The sound had been, perhaps, some child turning in her sleep. (Of what did Regina dream?)

Then step on, silently, stealthily . . .

And indeed was not one's tread *always* of a pantherine stealth and elegance? Probably nothing—if one *were* to be observed—could be detected by way of departure from one's usual demeanour : merely Miss Mount tirelessly going about her métier; her unrelaxing concern for her charges . . . Except, of course, to the eye of one of her charges who *knew* . . . But to the uncomprehending eye there was nothing to shew . . . Not a frill at one's throat betrayed the pulse, the taut pulse, beneath; this tiger's claws (were you, desire, remorseless?) had scratched not the surface of a ruffle at one's breast . . .

A door opened.

Not Regina's: Antonia—though her hand was on it—had not yet turned the knob.

Royalty's then. No. A rose still shut, sleeping undisturbed through the night. (*She*, surely, simply did not dream.)

Eugénie Plash's, in fact.

It had stood for a full moment open: and then, just as Antonia turned towards it, closed.

Inutile to go on, since Eugénie knew.

Howl

. . . but silently: silently tip-toe back, past royalty's door. And then?

To Eugénie's door? Have with her des explications? an éclaircissement? Try perhaps, even, to perceive once again the lost charm?

No, elle me ferait une scène, Antonia thought, hating, above all things in life, scenes . . .

Or not, perhaps, above all things; merely equally with all things. I am tired. I am, even, old.

I am—utterly—excédée.

Back, then . . . simply, back . . . the way one had come.

In youth one had felt the fatigue du nord; was one now to be overtaken by the fatigue du midi as well?

Lasse, lasse . . . lasse . . .

VIII

'So PALE, my love.'

Naturally: one had barely slept.

'Try to take a little coffee, my love. Let Hetty hold the cup.'

Return to consciousness: of . . .

'Take just a little more, and then sleep again.'

'But, my——'

'Just for once your special class shall be cancelled, my love. No, Hetty insists. My love is not to wear herself out for royalty.'

'But can you . . . manage?'

'My love must rest.'

'No new worries?'

'Nothing Hetty can't cope with.'

'But . . . something?'

'My love, only the Plash girls. So ungrateful. If they *knew* how you—half the night——'

(If, rather, they hadn't known.)

'What is the matter with them?' Antonia asked. 'La grippe, yet?' (As though she had it in store for them.)

97

'No, still the sulks, but it seems contagious. Eugénie has it too, now. They have both shut themselves up in Eugénie's room, and refuse to come out. *So* ungrateful.'

'Qu'elles boudent', said Antonia, lying back.

'Quite so. They deserve no better. I will cook a special little luncheon for my beloved, and then she shall sleep again till after the siesta.'

Yet even after the siesta, even though one was *up* and, in one's frail (but by no means careless) fashion, dressed, one still felt lasse almost à mourir.

'My love . . .'

'You seem troubled, Hetty.'

'Well, principally, my dearest, about you.'

'And next?'

'Well, next . . .'

'The Plash girls?'

'Still shut in.'

'Then one need hardly worry. They can come to no mischief, surely, renfermées.'

'No. It is, rather, Fraise du Bois.'

'Too deep droguée?'

'Too shallowly. We are—o my poor Antonia—*running out*.'

'The delivery not made?'

'No . . . Thirty-six hours overdue.'

'With effects, no doubt, as when the Mistral is?'

'Exactly. My love puts it so well. I would not be worried for myself. It is—well—the presence of royalty.'

'Ah.' Whether or not lizards could bite, Fraise du Bois could. So she had attested, the last time she had been overextended ('I bear her no grudge; the poor thing wasn't herself') on—indeed, *in*, to the bone même—Hetty's hand. If it were to be, this time, royalty's . . .

'Surely, if you were to drive into town, Hetty, and interview the pharmacien——'

'Yes, I'm sure I could—enough, at least, *to tide us over*. But——'

'But?'

'It would mean leaving my poor tired beloved in charge.'

'If it must be . . .'

'You are so brave. But you are also so tired. I can see it in your dear face.'

'One's strength is often greater than one imagines, when it is called upon. The girls, I presume, can occupy themselves in the gardens? Or in their rooms?' (As well the two Plash girls, when one was so weary already, be out of sight.)

99

'Yes, but the strain——'

'I suppose I need not be precisely *in* the gardens? merely . . . available?'

'Let us hope no need will arise.'

'Let us hope . . . On the verandah, for example?'

'If you feel strong enough——'

'When one must . . .'

'I will run and set out your chair, and pull down the sunblind.'

Hot, hot afternoon, air shimmering like those twisted paper stalactites which either turn or seem to turn, mazy, almost soundless, almost a mist of heat about the pelouse (even royalty had abandoned the attempt to 'get up' a rounders game and had sought, somewhere among the deeps of the terracing, the shade) —mist suddenly split by a running figure, chrysanthemum-haired, running, running, stumbling, running on: towards the house; towards the verandah, indeed, and the stained-glass-tinted shade of the striped blind—Regina—running for her life, hands en porte-voix: 'Miss Mount! Miss Mount!'

What . . . passion, was it? bred of the torrid afternoon? what folly of publicity, then (o, this heat), but touching . . . One was (who had thought oneself, if not dead, vieillie)—one was stirred . . .

'Miss Mount!' (how charmingly out of breath; that spot to which my eyes and my desires have so often tended—how delicately, now, panting) 'Miss Mount! Royalty!'

*What* had overtaken royalty? (I feel myself turn pale: one does *feel* it: a draining . . .) Fallen? Bitten? Had Fraise, then, not *held out*?

'Dear child? What? Try to tell me.'

'The guêpe du midi.'

The guêpe.

'Well, then . . .'

Surely every head, no matter how heat-languid in what leafy retreat, must crane forward, the Plash heads crane out from their window above, Fraise du Bois, in heaven knew what extremity of need and the gardens, attend . . . Antonia, without parasol, without *gloves*, even, advancing into the gardens (had she not once already, for royalty, made the tour of them?); Antonia, the trepidant chrysanthemum-head at her side, stepping . . .

Royalty (for once in her life, a sensible act) ran to encounter her.

'I say—I thought I'd better *hurry*—they say you've only got twenty minutes——'

Useless to ask where the wasp had stung:
a crimson pilule, almost perceptibly enlarging,
burned on the royal décolletage (thank God,
nowhere more intimate): on—o, irony!—that
very spot which, on Regina Outre-Mer . . .

Let neither one's revulsion nor the arrow of
irony render tremulous one's aim. Staunch,
hands! Grip—firmly, *steadyingly*—the royal
shoulders; bend, lovely neck; down, proud
head . . . And now (brave): suck, suck, suck
(a bee at how plain a flower) suck (bitter tingling
of venom on the tongue) suck (my mouth full)
further yet . . . my lungs burst . . .

Letting royalty's shoulders go and turning
aside, Antonia (with more than ever the gesture
of a paysan in a third-class carriage) spat out
the poison into a pink hydrangea in the flower
bed. (I have never spat in a garden before.)

'I say—was my life really in danger?—how
jolly—But I say, how frightfully decent of you.'

'Miss Mount, Miss Mount, how brave you
are.'

'Regina, dear child, do not faint until Miss
Braid comes back.'

Accept, then, the dear child's arm to lean on,
as one was without one's parasol; return—had
one thought one was tired before? (one had
fortunately, and thanks to royalty's one sensibleness, not come really very far out); play,
perhaps, insofar as one was not too entirely

exhausted, like a languid lizard, over the dear little wrist-knob as one leaned on it . . .

'Miss Mount!' (Was there no end?) 'Miss Mount! Miss Mount!'

The Plash girls; precipitate; scrambling.

'One had understood you to be sulking.'

But now all hurry; a request for permission to post a packet.

'Miss Braid is not here to drive you to the post.'

They could, they protested, go alone; would speak to no one; 'word of honour, Miss Mount' (thus Eugénie; once so charming in eager mood; now one would be glad to be quit . . .)

What matter, when one was so weary, if their packet should be positively addressed to a sailor? (Thought too compromising to surmise what it might contain.) One could not care what assignations they might be keeping. (One gave a wearied but not unbecoming haussement.) Qu'elles partent. Hetty would be glad, at least, to have their sulks cured.

Besides, better (if one was now going to request Regina's arm up to one's boudoir, to rest a little; and who could say what, in the after-impress of violent emotion, might, on both sides . . . ?) that Eugénie Plash should be out of earshot as well as sight.

So: qu'elles partent. 'Your arm, dear child.' (Your dear, knob-decorative arm.)

And yet, cunningly as one had arranged to give oneself, as it were, feu vert . . . Yet, as one frailly let oneself be helped upstairs ('Go higher') and looked down at the child's summery décolletage, the memory (of that very spot, but on another breast), the re-vivified taste of the poison . . .

Is my whole life, then, envenomed? Am I to live in desert for ever?

Well not, perhaps, for ever.

Tomorrow, perhaps; one hoped.

But now—*could* one? No; one was dead, dead . . . 'Leave me, my dear, here' (at the door of my room). One was—one sank down— épuisée.

***

Hetty, returned, wept over Antonia's bravery.

(And the other would have wept, too; and more than wept: but I feel drained, drained.)

'But, my darling—are you *sure* you spat it all out?'

'Yes, yes . . .'

'And rinsed your mouth after?'

'Yes.' (It was *too* gross: like prophylactic measures after some too gross to be précisé sexual act.) 'And then I drank a glass of ouzo.'

'Of ouzo, my love?'

'Since it behaves like a disinfectant when one pours in the water, let it disinfect . . .'

'Ah, my love. My darling, rest. Try to rest. Heaven send you are not poisoned.'

Only my imagination, only my imagination . . .

IX

OVERNIGHT, unnoticed, the pink hydrangea in the flower bed—not withered: turned blue. Who should notice? A blue hydrangea is a perfectly commonplace sight. Only Antonia might have remarked the unnaturally sudden change. But she seldom went into the gardens.

No doubt in time it would gradually grow pink again.

X

WOMEN like Hetty were natural believers in witchcraft (even, perhaps, involuntary practitioners: had her fears *induced* the guêpe . . . ?) Now the guêpe had stung, Hetty seemed assured the désenvôutement had been performed: chance had shot its malign bolt and been—so bravely—warded off; the School could continue . . .

No doubt because Hetty was more détendue, a certain pleasantly subdued, a bee-like (the guêpes seemed to have retired from the heat) activity was re-established. Antonia from her window seemed to look down on the normal pleasures of a hot Sunday morning, surging, with a not unpleasing tension, towards the luncheon bell. Even in herself Antonia sensed a certain return—was that not the black President's daughter glinting through a juniper? . . . The Plash girls, at whom, despite one's long sight, one need not look too closely, restored to the gardens (Sylvie even consenting to 'pick a side' to play against royalty); Fraise du Bois, correctly dosed, (had Hetty remembered to counsel her not to go too headstrong at the new supply?) flat in an asparagus trench; the Badessa *waddling* . . .

Only Regina Outre-Mer, at the verge of the grenouillère, wept . . .

She wept, no doubt, for Antonia's neglect.

(But could one help oneself, if one's sensibilities were so acute?)

Yet: poor child.

She wept as prettily as a willow.

Could it be one was stirred, again, into . . . ?

No doubt this wound, too, in time would pass: tout, after all, passe: and presently one might resume . . .

Meanwhile, the President's daughter—perhaps they were not so cold but that one might provoke . . . ? One's imagination, stimulated by the half veiling of juniper leaves, might care to toy . . . Picture the girl wholly clad in juniper leaves—or, rather, not wholly clad, but clad in nothing else: or in peacock feathers? Or one would still like to try sapphires, if one could decide how to affix them. Curious how the sight of this girl always set one's mind to *experiment*. Now that she appeared, by happy accident, to be dressed wholly in juniper leaves (with, here and there, a berry) one's mind naturally wished . . . One would like, bref, to lay hands on her—just to make her all of a piece . . . to re-dress, perhaps, those two long locks (il lui faut une coiffure qui aille avec) . . .

Or was it not (lasse that I am of sophistication) the natural, the indeed horticultural, coiffure of Regina Outre-Mer which drew the eye?

Perhaps: well,—soon. Antonia turned (one could not always be playing) to her Sunday devoir, shook out her newspaper and—sat, médusée.

The entire front page was giving to a photograph of Antonia apparently kissing—just above the bosom—royalty.

Naufrage.

'Étrange Affection entre Professeur et Élève', said the gross black headline.

Étrange it would have been indeed, had it existed.

It was not hard to trace the trajectory (the word: could bullets have done worse?) of the shot to Eugénie Plash's window.

'Hetty——' No: futile to enquire whether Sylvie Plash had handed in her camera. Obviously, she had not. One did not wish one's conversation, even in extremities, to be obvious.

Étrange Affection entre . . . He was, in his way, this sub-editor, classical: 'Embrassez-moi pour l'amour du grec.' (At least one had never wasted one's time trying to teach royalty *Greek*.)

Embrassez-moi . . . Ah, Regina, Regina . . . Quelle folie.

What, then, to do?

Nothing. Nothing to do. Nothing to be done.

(One might—opportunity now lost for ever—have taught *Regina* Greek. A few poems of Sappho, perhaps? . . .)

At least the horrible child had focussed the appareil quite well (fortunate that one had not, in effect, progressed very far from the house: the child was, after all, only an amateur). One had been caught (*caught!*) in—that so tender stoop—a not unbecoming attitude.

But even that . . (Regina, Regina.)

XI

'I SAY. Get me some background on this Mount woman, will you?'

'Right. I'll look through the files.'

'Won't be in the files. You'll have to tap the old boy network.'

'Right.'

'Find out if she's *that kind of woman*.'

'Right you are. If she's communist, you mean?'

'No, no, no, no, no' (agacé).

The *Canard Enchâiné* reproduced the photograph, much smaller (less becoming: something of distinction was lost) with the comment
'Mâitresse d'école?'

'Got it?'

'I'll *say*.'

'Well, look. Let me have the salient facts in memorandum form.'

'I don't know that I can *write them down*.'

The Palace, as it turned out, waited for no memoranda. They telephoned immediately ('Miss Mount is not available. She is indisposed'): orders had been radioed to Commander Curl; he was to come, in person, at once; let, meanwhile, royalty's thirty-one bags be packed.

XII

'MY BELOVED' (twenty-three bags had been packed) 'there is no need for you to sit up. There is no need for you to see him, even.'

'It is my wish to.'

'At least let me be with you, to support you.'

'Mine be the interview, since mine was the —error.'

'It is so late, my love, and you are so saddened already. Must you stay awake all night? Let me at least make you——'

'You have the packing to do. I will see him alone.'

'Antonia, you know I will never abandon you. I will support you through—everything.'

Ah, but if we have no means of support? Les

Plash had been expelled, of course (I blame my-self; if I had properly looked at Sylvie Plash's face, I should never have admitted them in the first place). But would one, in time, find oneself regretting them? They were, at least, pupils. Regina Outre-Mer had been withdrawn (Howl, howl): the President's daughter—gone in a flash of damson-blue bloom: the Badessa likewise, with a flash of daisy (though her one could not, try as one would, regret) . . . All, all gone . . . (Even Fraise du Bois—whose guardians, in-continent, had come for her at quite the wrong stage of the day—carted off, inert . . .)

Curiously enough there had been, by the very post that brought the withdrawals, several new applications. Antonia was confident there would be more still. Strange reversal, Antonia firm, Hetty faltering.

('Do you think, my belovedest, they will have quite the same—be quite the type of girl we want?'

'I think', Antonia had replied, 'they will be in some ways even *more* the . . .')

﷯

Hetty hesitant outside the door, a cup of

warm milk in her hand: twenty-nine bags
had been packed: she must be allowed (without lèse-majesté) to spare a moment to
Antonia.

Yet she dared not go in.

What agonies of humiliating interview the
poor beloved must be undergoing with the jolly
(and my love is so delicate) Commander.
Humiliation: and my poor love is so proud.

* * *

'My colleague would, I feel sure, prepare
some *warm milk* if you preferred. But, I felt, a
*sailor* . . . Indeed, I, too, I confess . . .'

(Tonight one seemed to be favouring—and
one had been on the point of becoming certain
one's taste had permanently settled for the
yellow—the green Chartreuse.)

* * *

Hetty descended to the kitchen, re-heated the
milk and carried the cup upstairs again. (One

more suitcase to go: but it was Antonia who
needed sustaining . . .)

'I say—I didn't expect—I *say*, Miss Mount,
Antonia—(May I call you Antonia? I mean,
hadn't I *better*? *now*?)'

'Dear' (is it I who from my girls or my girls
who from me have caught this faiblesse for
sailors?) 'boy . . .'

(Those knees, so—though touchingly—absurd
when they had been the only things bare, were
quite vindicated now that . . .)

'I must say, I never—I can't get over it— (o,
I SAY)—I mean, I was told—I didn't—not *this*
kind of wo——'

'Yet one must from time to time permit oneself' (ah, the relief!) 'refreshment . . . before
. . .' (*before*, thought Antonia, the new girls:
one would like to be at one's most relaxed to
meet them) . . . 'One is surely entitled to . . .
recuperation . . . after . . .'—*after*, one meant,
though one did not like to say so (in case the
poor dear man should, however mistakenly,
feel himself to be being *used*), after the tensions,
the hysteria, the really at times too insupport-

able emotional *fraught*-ness, of these all-female institutions.

❧❧❧

Ah, my poor love—if only one dared go in (Hetty skimmed another skin off the milk and tried to keep the cup cosy between her hands). What agony of a frozen interview must be proceeding behind the door one dare not broach. One could tell: the voices were stilled, now, to silence: no doubt all that could be said had been said, leaving only the embarrassment—ah, torment!—of the coarse man's moral disapproval. Only, from time to time, a moment's moan (of my beloved's via crucis, no doubt): a murmur from the Commander (was he trying, had he the effrontery, to excuse himself?)

My *poor* darling—— Her moan, again; o, her torment; o, her humiliation.

## Robert Ferro
## THE BLUE STAR

Peter first meets Chase Walker in a Florence pension.
Both are young Americans, in Europe to satisfy not onl
hungers of the spirit but also more pressing needs o
the flesh. Their travels together take them fror
clandestine meetings in dark alleyways and on moonl
riverbanks, to amorous intrigues in Italian palaces, to
final voyage on *The Blue Star*, a yacht whose passenger
seek to make all their dreams and fantasies com
true . . .

"One of the most accomplished writers in English"
Edmund White.

"Superb taste and style . . . A writer of outstandin
power and promise" – *Publishers Weekly*.

"Authentic fiction . . . a treasure. This surprising, sa
funny story is recounted with irony and a wise sense o
the ambiguities of relationship. The characters ar
drawn vividly, the prose is lean, the structure of th
work solid" – *The Advocate*.

ISBN 0 85449 041 8 (pbk) UK £4.95

**ay Dick**
**HE SHELF**

"he shelf" is a repository in the coroner's office where assandra's letters to Anne had first been lodged – as ell as that other, unposted letter found in Anne's andbag. It was all so long ago – back in the 1960s – but ass has not been able to forget the passion Anne igendered in her; their brief affair; and the mystery iat surrounded it.

tecalls writers like Elizabeth Bowen, Rosamund ehmann and Elizabeth Taylor. What these writers ive in common with Miss Dick is a willingness to ...rd the intricacies of love, the shifting patterns of ht and shade in the relationship of one person to the her, as being of prime importance. The stylish onomy of Kay Dick's writing places her firmly in that adition. It is a book you are not likely to forget" – llan Massie, *The Scotsman*.

heme, manner and writing evoke Colette" – *Daily elegraph*.

tour de force, powerful in its evocation of rela- inships and the gradations of passion. This work aces Kay Dick in the same category of sensibility as an Rhys, Katherine Mansfield and Ford Maddox Ford" Gillian Freeman.

BN 0 85449 002 7 (pbk) UK £3.50/US $6.50

**Francis King**
**THE MAN ON THE ROCK**

Like many destitute and unemployed young men
post-war Greece, Spiros Polymerides has only
natural cunning and good looks to help him survive
con-man, petty thief and parasite, he moves relentle
from victim to victim: Irvine, the repressed gay
who befriends him; Helen, the wealthy, middle-a
Englishwoman with whom he has an affair; Kiki
Greek shipping heiress he is eventually to marry.
by one he exploits and betrays them all – onl
discover that the final victim is himself.

"Reveals clearly Mr King's capacity for getting ins
character. In this novel, he has succeeded not on
making a remarkably understanding study of
relation between exploiter and exploited, bu
presenting an extremely vivid picture of contempo
Greece" – *Time and Tide.*

"Few English novelists have written with more m
and assurance" – *Spectator.*

ISBN 0 85449 022 1 (pbk) UK £3.95/US $7.95